Hello, Reader!

There's a big sale on roller skates.
"People came from far and wide.
Even people who had never tried...
The Bensons were out for their
afternoon stroll.
Then they decided to go out and roll!"
Soon the whole town is on skates!

Roller

Te:

Calmenso
Roller
p.
Summ
the pizza

[1. Rol
PZ8.C13
[E]—dc2

12 11 10

This book is a gift from
Immanuel Lutheran Church
Jackson, Michigan,
the church where everyone is welcome.

Worship times: Saturday, 6:00 p.m.
Sunday, 10:00 a.m.

God's Blessings!

elley.

n to Pete

92-3657
CIP
AC

6 7/9
23

Printed in the U.S.A.
First Scholastic printing, October 1992

Skates!

By Stephanie Calmenson
Illustrated by True Kelley

Cartwheel
·B·O·O·K·S· ®

SCHOLASTIC INC.
New York   Toronto   London   Auckland   Sydney

Early one morning
in a small sleepy town,
six trucks rumbled up
and boxes came down.

Sam Skipper called out
as the trucks drove away,
"Two boxes were all
that I needed today!"

He counted the boxes.
There were fifty-two.
He sat down and said,
"Now what will I do?"

Soon an idea
popped into Sam's head.
He made up a sign
and here's what it said:
BIG SALE TODAY ON
ROLLER SKATES!

People came
from far and wide.
There were even people
who never had tried
to get around on
roller skates.

The Bensons were out
for their afternoon stroll.
Then they decided
to go out and roll!
The Bensons got four pairs of
roller skates.

Joe, the mail carrier, said,
"Skates will be great!
I can go fast,
and the mail won't be late!"
He delivered the mail on
roller skates.

Anna Lee
knew what to do.
She strapped on one.
She strapped on two.
She jumped and twirled on her
roller skates.

Pizza stays hot
when you soar down the street.
For delivering pizza,
skates can't be beat!
Watch out for Pete on his
roller skates.

Shopping for supper
is no longer a chore.
Martha fills up her basket
as she zips through the store.
It's fun to shop on
roller skates.

Sam, Sue, and Sal like
how it feels when
Mommy and Daddy
take them out on wheels.
Someday they will *all* go on
roller skates!

Be careful, Billy.
Don't go too fast.
Your ice-cream cone
will never last.
It's hard to eat ice cream on
roller skates.

Jordan's daddy
drove to work in his car,
even though his office
was not very far.
Now Daddy is cool on his
roller skates.

Jill's job walking dogs
became a breeze.
She rolled along
the street with ease.
The dogs pull Jill on her
roller skates.

Now in this lively town,
all the people agree
that life is as easy
as it can be...

when everyone rides on
roller skates!